Every Little Bit Olive Tran

Library and Archives Canada Cataloguing in Publication

Title: Every little bit Olive Tran / Phuong Truong.
Names: Truong, Phuong, author.
Description: Series statement: Olive Tran series | Text chiefly in English; some text in Vietnamese.
Identifiers: Canadiana (print) 20240460308 | Canadiana (ebook) 20240462815 | ISBN 9781772604139 (softcover) | ISBN 9781772604146 (EPUB)
Subjects: LCGFT: Novels.
Classification: LCC PS8639.R86 E94 2025 | DDC jC813/.6—dc23

Copyright © 2025 Phuong Truong
Cover and illustrations by Christine Wei
Printed and bound in Canada

Second Story Press gratefully acknowledges the support of the Ontario Arts Council and the Canada Council for the Arts for our publishing program. We acknowledge the financial support of the Government of Canada through the Canada Book Fund.

Second Story Press expressly prohibits the use of *Every Little Bit Olive Tran* in connection with the development of any software program, including, without limitation, training a machine learning or generative artificial intelligence (AI) system.

Published by
SECOND STORY PRESS
20 Maud Street, Suite 401
Toronto, ON M5V 2M5
www.secondstorypress.ca

Every Little Bit Olive Tran

Second Story Press

PHUONG TRUONG

To Mom and Dad for everything, and to Tu for making so many of my school lunches.

Chapter 1

T-minus two days until I'm officially ten years old. In other words, two days until freedom!

It's all I can think about as I watch the clock on the wall, willing it to move just a little faster, itching to hear the jangling bell that signals the end of another school day. I'll be the first in my class to turn ten and the first to finally be able to walk to and from school by myself. Most importantly, I'll be able to pop into the convenience store—Kandy Korner, don't even get me started on the spelling of that name!—any time I want. I can already imagine the fizzy, refreshing soda, the puckering bite of the sour keys, the smooth sweetness of the chocolate bars. *Sigh*.

"That's it, folks!" Mr. Chu announces. "Time to pack up and mosey on into the sunset. I'll see y'all in the mornin'." Ever since we voted to watch *Toy Story* for our monthly class movie, Mr. Chu's fancied himself a cowboy. We're watching *Mary Poppins* next, though. Oh, boy.

I tidy my desk, grab my backpack and jacket from my locker, and head outside to meet Mom. There's a bit of a chill in the air still, but the sun is shining. My favorite kind of weather. The schoolyard is an organized chaos, with teachers dismissing their students, and kids zooming toward their parents or the jungle gym for a last few minutes of playtime before heading home.

As usual, Mom's waiting for me under the big maple tree. She wears SPF 70 and avoids the sun like the plague. I bet when she gets older, she'll wear one of those giant visors that Grandma and all her friends love. Hmmm, maybe a giant visor would be a good Mother's Day gift. I'll have to tuck that idea away for later.

She catches Mr. Chu's eye and gives him a wave. That's my cue. I make my way toward her when a little girl races by and trips right in front of me. Luckily, I manage to catch her before she falls. It turns out to be Sammy, my friend Josh's little sister.

"Thanks, Olive!" she yells as she continues on her way, the close call already forgotten. I smile. All in a day's work for an almost-ten-year-old.

"How was your day, kiddo?" asks Mom as she takes the bag from my shoulder and transfers it to her own for the short walk home. She doesn't need to, but it's nice that she does.

"It was good. I liked the egg salad sandwich you packed me for lunch. I could have done without the carrot sticks. Oh, and my entire class played a huge game of tag in the field."

"I see that lunch is still your favorite subject," she laughed. "You know the drill, tell me something that you learned today."

I wave goodbye to Mia, Penny, and Ella—my besties—as we pass the fence that

surrounds the schoolyard. Hmmm, surely I must have learned something today. I have to dig deep to finally come up with a fact that would count as new. "Mr. Chu does a really bad country western accent."

Mom rolls her eyes. "Try again."

Hrmph. "In science, we learned that the four types of clouds are cumulus, cirrus, stratus, and nimbus."

"Much better. And what's the difference between all these kinds of clouds?" she asks.

I roll my eyes right back at her. "Mom, we've talked about this. The game is *one* thing I've learned. Besides, my still-developing brain can only take in so much information each day. You wouldn't want me to stuff *too* many facts in there. I could overload! Spontaneously combust!"

Mom taps the side of my head. "You know you won't be able to use that excuse forever."

"Do you think we'll still be playing Tell Me Something You Learned Today by then?"

"You know what? I really hope so."

Chapter 2

As soon as we walk in the door, I can smell that Bà Nội has been up to something in the kitchen. I take off my shoes, exchange them for slippers, and zoom over to give my grandma a peck on the cheek. And to sneak a peek at what's cooking.

"Hi, Bà Nội. Mmmm, *gòi cuốn*."

"Hi, *Con*. Sit. Eat."

My older brother, Ben, is already seated and completely focused on demolishing his food. Bà Nội takes two plump summer rolls

from the mountain she's already prepared and sets them on a small plate for me. Sliced pork and shrimp, noodles, lettuce, cucumber, and mint are all packaged together in a softened rice paper wrapper. Dinner is still a couple of hours away, so a small taster is definitely in order.

"Thank you!" I pick up the roll, dip it in some tangy peanut sauce, and take a giant bite. "Yummy!"

"Olive, after you're finished your snack, do any homework you have, please," says Mom. "Bà Nội wants to go to the Asian market tonight after dinner, and if you want to go too, I want all your assignments done."

"Yessss! I love the Asian market!" And lucky for me, I don't even have any homework tonight!

The Asian supermarket is my happy place. It's got Kandy Korner beat, hands down. There's just so much stuff that you can't find anywhere else. The bakery has sweet buns filled with red bean, custard, or taro—my favorite. And it's got *the* best snack section. Sweet mango jellies and creamy milk candies. Potato chips in fun flavors like Peking duck or spicy crab. And the fruit! Tart mangosteens and spiky durians. Durians are known as the stinkiest fruit in the world and have even been banned in some hotels and airports because of it. I'll have to remember that fact for Mom's next pop quiz. But once you get past the prickly outer shell and into the pillowy yellow fruit, they are creamy and delicious. Grandma says that the fruit in Vietnam tastes a million times better, but it still tastes pretty good to me.

"Doesn't Bà Nội usually go shopping during the day? How come we're going so late?" I ask.

Mom exchanges a look with my grandma. "Well, you know Mrs. Ly? A couple of days ago, she was in Chinatown and she had a bit of an accident. So, Bà Nội just wants to be careful."

"What kind of accident?" I ask. "Is she okay?"

"She fell in the street," Mom says quickly. She busies herself with wiping what looks like an already clean counter. Bà Nội always cleans as she cooks and expects everyone to keep her kitchen tidy.

"Mom," Ben scoffs, "c'mon. She didn't just fall. She was pushed."

I gasp. "Why would anyone push Mrs. Ly? She's just a little old lady." Mrs. Ly is the sweetest. I don't think I've ever seen her without a smile on her face. She doesn't speak that much English, so our conversations are pretty short, but she always gives me a candy from the stash in her purse. But most importantly, Mrs. Ly is tiny! She's not much taller than me!

"I don't know." Mom is turned away from me, now putting some leftovers in the fridge, but I see her shoulders droop a little. "Luckily, there were lots of people around to help her, but her wrist is a little bruised, and she's pretty shaken up. I think it was just a random accident."

Ben rinses his plate and puts it in the dishwasher. "Sure, Mom. It was totally random."

Why do I get the feeling that it was anything but?

Chapter 3

The next morning at school passes in a blur of the usual things. A little math, a touch of spelling (one of my best subjects!), and the mayhem of music. We've just started learning how to play the recorder, and while I love my classmates, I'll be the first to admit that we suck. Half the class hits the wrong note, the other half gets the right one...just at the wrong time. Altogether, we're making one giant racket. On the bright side, we can only get better!

Lunch time is when I really start to wake up. Today I've got ham and cheese wraps, apple sauce, a couple of cookies, and more of the dreaded carrot sticks. I did get some bonus leftover summer rolls to snack on too, enough to share with my friends.

"Nice! I love it when your granny's in charge of dinner," says Mia as she munches on a roll.

"Well, she's gonna be making stuff for my birthday party, and I've invited the whole class, so there will be a ton of food. You can eat your heart out in a few days!" I grin.

Mia and Penny high-five each other.

My birthday is on a Friday this year, so I'm having my party the next day. Mom has booked Sky's the Limit!, a trampoline park, and I've invited everyone in my class. I got to choose the theme, and by theme, I mean food, 'cause that's all I really care about. So, we're going with Tastes of Asia! Chinese potstickers, Japanese sushi, Korean japchae, and of course, Grandma's famous spring rolls. But knowing Mom, we'll also have a cheese pizza, just in case.

We finish eating, pack up our lunch bags, and head outside. "What do we have going today?" I ask. It's another sunny day, and abandoned jackets are heaped in a pile by the fence. Why do parents always insist on jackets when they know we're not going to wear them?

"I heard there's a big four square tournament," says Ella. "We're going to use both of the courts, so everyone should get a chance. If you get knocked out of one game, you can try your luck at the other one. The last ones standing when the bell rings are the winners."

I'm pretty amazing at four square, so I think I've got this in the bag. The only other person in my class who may be a challenge is Josh. I've known Josh since kindergarten and he's my best boy friend. And by that, I mean my best friend who is a boy, *not* boyfriend. Anyway, we've been in and out of each other's houses since we were little.

The games are already underway by the time we get to the courts, so I line up to play at the one Josh is already dominating. First Erin, then Tim, then Curtis get eliminated. It's finally my turn.

Freddy sends the ball flying to my square, and I redirect it toward Josh's. It wasn't that hard a pass, so I'm surprised when Josh bobbles the ball. He leaves the court quickly, and Sasha takes his spot. I turn my focus back to the game and return every ball that comes my way. When the bell rings, signaling the end of lunch and our tournament, I bump fists with the other winners.

I look around for Josh but don't see him anywhere. It's too bad that he got knocked out so early. I was hoping to get a good match going with him. I didn't even get a chance to razz him for losing!

Chapter 4

When I get home from school that afternoon, I find a plate of sliced oranges that Bà Nội has set out for me. I carry my snack to the dining room where Ben is surrounded by markers and other art supplies that he has pilfered from my room.

"What are you doing?" I ask as I take a seat at the table.

"Hey, don't get orange juice all over my stuff," he says, creating a protective barrier over his work with his arms. "I'm working on some posters for the Asian Students Association."

I stick out my tongue at him but move over a bit as asked. The Asian Students Association is pretty cool. They have movie nights every other week, and they show things like anime or wuxia films. They also celebrate Asian holidays like Lunar New Year and Chuseok, the Mid-Autumn Festival. A big part of these holidays is the food, so the club learned how to make long-life noodles and yummy dumplings. So, obviously, I'll be joining the group, too, when I get to high school.

"'If you feel unsafe and would like someone to walk with you to class, contact the Asian Students Association,'" I read off the poster that Ben has created using thick black letters. "Why would anyone need someone to walk them to school? Oh, and in case you forgot, *I* can start walking to school by myself tomorrow. I can't wait!"

"Oh, is it your birthday tomorrow? I wouldn't have known, except you've mentioned it at least twice a day, every day, for the last month." Brothers, am I right? "Some of the kids at my school have run into problems lately." He avoids looking at me and seems to concentrate pretty fiercely on forming some basic letters on his poster.

Hmmm, what is he hiding? "What kind of problems?"

He sighs. "I don't think Mom wanted me to mention this to you, but I think you should know. A couple of kids were targeted by a guy carrying buckets of nasty stuff.

He just tossed it at them for no reason. Some kids have started carrying umbrellas all the time, ready to block any stream thrown their way."

"Ewww, gross." I wrinkle my nose.

"Some other kids have reported people yelling at them, telling them to 'Go home! Go back to where you came from!'"

What? I don't get it. Why would people tell kids on their way to school to go home? The confusion must have been clear on my face because Ben puts down his marker.

"Olive, all of the kids that were targeted have been Asian," he explains. "That's why I think you should know. If you're going to be walking by yourself, you should be vigilant. Make sure you're paying attention to your surroundings."

"But that's so unfair!" I cry. "Why just the Asian kids? What did we do?"

"Nothing!" Ben says angrily and roughly runs his hands through his short hair. "Life's not always fair. It's just something we have to deal with, something we've always had to deal with."

Always? Ben's been old enough to go out on his own for years now. Has he been dealing with this stuff all this time? "What about you?" I ask. "Has anything ever happened to you?"

"Sure." He shrugs. "Luckily, it wasn't too big a deal. Some people called me 'Chinaman' and pulled at the corners of their eyes. I just ignored them, and they went away. I told Mom what happened, and she said the same thing happened to her when she was young."

Why hadn't I heard any of this? It makes me think about Mrs. Ly. "Do you think that's why Mrs. Ly was pushed the other day? Because she's Asian?"

Ben's silence seems to confirm my suspicions. "Maybe the Asian Students Association could offer to walk with older people too, not just other students? If they need to go to the market like Mrs. Ly and Bà Nội?"

"That's not a bad idea. I'll bring it up when I hand in my posters." He smiles and ruffles my hair. I let it slide this time and make sure to remember that he borrowed my markers without asking. That'll come in handy next time I need a favor.

Chapter 5

It's my big day. I'm ten! I jump out of bed and snatch open the curtain. The sun is up, and the sky is clear. It's going to be a perfect day, I can already tell.

I slide on my favorite jeans and green sweatshirt. Perfect. I brush through my hair and bangs and get it all nice and smooth, no flyaways, on my first try. Perfect. Heading downstairs, I sit at the breakfast table. My mom slides a plate of blueberry pancakes with whipped cream and maple syrup in front of me. The same birthday breakfast I've requested every year for as long as I can remember. Perfect.

"Happy birthday, sweetheart!" she says and kisses the top of my head.

"Happy birthday, Con," says Grandma. She gives me a squeeze and slides a red envelope in front of me.

I wiggle in excitement and open the envelope. Twenty whole dollars! "Thank you, Bà Nội!"

I've got a date with a certain convenience store after school, and this is definitely going to come in handy.

Ben, who's *not* a morning person, cracks a giant yawn as he sits down at the table. "Happy birthday. Here," he grunts and hands me a card. He perks up a little when Mom places his breakfast in front of him.

"What's this?" I ask. His card contains a small ticket he's made himself out of colored paper and magic markers. He's been in my art supplies again—that's two favors he owes me! "A coupon?"

"We all know your favorite gifts are things you can eat," he says around a mouthful of pancakes. "This coupon entitles you to dinner and a movie. With me. You can choose the food and the movie."

Huh, it's a surprisingly good present. Okay, I'll forgive him for using my markers. Back to one favor in the bank. "Wow, thanks, Ben!"

"Redeemable only when I don't have any other plans, of course," he quickly adds.

Mom sits down at the table with her own stack of pancakes and a cup of coffee. I love the smell of coffee, but Mom let me have a sip of hers once and it was disgusting. "Olive, are you sure you don't want me to walk you to school today?" she asks.

"*Mommmmmm*," I whine, "it's only eight minutes away. I think I can manage it."

"I know, I know. You're ten!" she says with a huff. "But just because you *can* walk to school on your own, doesn't mean you have to. I've heard that some people actually like spending time with their mothers."

I drag the last bit of pancake through the sticky mess of syrup and cream. I'd lick my plate clean if my mom would allow it. "I think I'm good, Mom. Oh, and remember, you don't have to pick me up after school either."

"It's the end of an era," Mom says with a bit of a quiver in her voice. She clears her throat. "Try not to go too crazy at Kandy Korner."

Chapter 6

This is it. My first solo walk to school. Yes, I've walked this exact route with my mom more times than I could count. And yes, it's only four blocks away. But it's just the first step on my path to independence. Today, I walk to school. Tomorrow, I'm off to college. And shortly after that, I'll be president! I'll figure out the details later.

I skip down the steps and turn to wave at Mom who, as expected, is peeking from behind the curtain in our front window. "Bye, Mom!" I call out. The curtain swishes closed.

I take a deep breath. I'm still only in front of my own house, but I already feel like a different person. I couldn't wait to start my first solo trek, so I'm pretty early, and stroll leisurely down the street. The front gardens haven't started blooming yet, and I get a clear view of Mrs. Mac's grumpy-faced gnome. *Cheer up, Sven*, I think. *It's my birthday!*

It doesn't take long for me to notice how quiet it is. That's weird, where are all the other kids on their way to school? Where are the dogs getting their morning walks? I'm the only person outside. I guess I left *really* early. And Mom usually keeps up a steady stream of conversation, telling me about her plans for the day or reminding me of after-school activities. All I can hear today are a few birds and the thoughts in my own head.

I'm excited to get to school and to squeeze every little bit that I can out of my birthday. Everyone will have to be extra nice to me today. It's an unwritten birthday rule. Maybe I can even choose what game we play in gym class!

A car door slams, and I jump a little. I look over my shoulder and see a man I don't recognize walking along the sidewalk behind me. He doesn't look suspicious, but everything Ben told me yesterday creeps into my head. How some of the older kids have been attacked just for being Asian. By complete strangers! And there's a stranger right behind me! I've always felt safe in my neighborhood, but maybe those kids did, too. I take another quick peek back. There's still lots of space between me and the man, and I don't think he's following me, but what if he is? I pick up my pace. I try to shake off my nervousness, but my heart is racing. I walk a little faster. And a little faster—until I'm practically flying down the sidewalk.

"Olive!" shouts a voice that I am relieved to recognize. I look to my left and find Mia and her father approaching from one of the streets that branches off mine. I skid to a stop with only one more block to go.

"Why are you running so fast?" Mia asks. "The bell doesn't go for another ten minutes!"

I wipe away some of the sweat that's gathered at the top of my forehead. "Oh, you know," I say, not wanting to admit that I was scared. Mom seems to have eyes and ears everywhere, and I don't want her deciding that I'm not ready to go to school by myself after all. "Just getting in some practice. It'll be track and field tryouts before we know it!"

Since I've never mentioned track before, Mia looks unconvinced, but she just shrugs. "Hey, happy birthday! I can't wait for your party tomorrow. It's going to be so much fun!"

"Thanks, Mia!" Without my noticing, the sidewalks have filled with familiar faces, and my earlier fear seems silly. "I think almost everyone is coming. We got the deluxe package, so we've got the entire place to ourselves for three whole hours! It's going to be epic!"

We arrive in the schoolyard, and Mr. Ahmad peels off to chat with a group of parents clutching their coffees. Mia and I meet up with Penny and Ella to discuss the latest episode of *Magic Sparkle Fairy Ponies*. We've just gotten to the cliff-hanger ending—TWINS! GASP!—when we have to line up and go inside. Conversation definitely to be continued.

Chapter 7

The morning announcements are usually reserved for notices about clubs and sports teams, except for one special thing: birthday shout-outs! And today, that shout-out is for me!

"Happy birthday to...um...Olive Tran," crackles over our PA system.

The class breaks out in cheers and clapping. My besties have snuck in some noisemakers and are honking loudly, paper tubes shooting from their mouths with every blow. Blood rushes to my face with pleasure as I look around the room. Someone has even written "Happy Birthday, Olive!" on the chalkboard. But on the far side of the room, Josh sits slumped over at his desk, looking down at his folded hands. I wonder if he's feeling okay.

Lessons begin and I miss my chance to ask him about it. This day just keeps getting better when I find out we're doing a class spelling bee. Most of the class groans, but I love words, I love reading, and I love spelling. As I expected, I make it to the last round. "Olive, your word is *physical*," says Mr. Chu in his hushed announcer voice, no trace of the country twang he's already used way too much.

"Physical," I repeat. I've read and used this word a million times, but for some reason, I'm drawing a blank. "Physical. F-I-S-I-C-A-L?"

"Ooh, sorry, Olive," says Mr. Chu. "That is incorrect. It's spelled P—"

"H-Y-S-I-C-A-L. Urgh, I knew that," I groan and smack my forehead with my hand. Ah well, you can't win 'em all, I guess. My special day is a little less perfect, but still pretty good.

"That makes Josh today's grand spelling bee champ. Everyone give Josh a big ol' round of applause!" says Mr. Cowboy Chu.

We all clap for Josh and cheer even more when we hear it's time for lunch. I'm just about ready to head out with Mia, Penny, and Ella when Josh taps me on the shoulder.

"Can I speak to you a minute, Olive?" he asks.

"Sure. I'll catch up with you guys in a bit," I tell my friends. "Hey, are you okay? You looked like you weren't feeling so good this morning."

"I'm fine," he says. "Sorry you didn't win the spelling bee. That was a hard word you got."

I laugh. "No, it wasn't. I just froze. You won fair and square." I wait for Josh to continue, but he just stands there, looking in my direction but not quite at me. "Was that all you wanted to talk to me about?"

"Actually, no." Josh clutches his lunch bag so tightly, I worry that his lunch will be crunched into a ball by the time he gets to it. "It's your party. I don't think I'll be able to come."

"Oh no!" I say. Josh's mom was one of the first to send in her RSVP. "How come?"

"It's kinda hard to explain," he says, seeming to struggle to find the right words. "I just don't think it's a great idea for me to go."

I don't understand at all. It's not a great idea? Josh and I have been friends forever and he loves trampolining. It's one of the reasons why I wanted to have my party at Sky's the Limit! "Did I do something wrong? Are you mad at me?" I ask.

"No, it's not you." After a long pause, he continues, "It's my dad. He's going through a tough time right now." He keeps his head bowed, like he doesn't want to look at me, which makes absolutely no sense.

I put my hand on his shoulder. "Is your dad okay? Is he sick? Do you have to stay home to take care of him?"

Josh seems to wilt, to get smaller somehow. "It's not that." He takes a deep breath. "Remember how my grandma got really sick during the pandemic?"

Oh no, not his grandma. "Yes, but she's okay now, right? She got better?"

"Yeah, she's mostly better now," he says slowly, "but she still has a cough that she can't seem to get rid of. Then I heard my parents talking the other night, and my dad may lose his job because his company just lost a big contract to another company in Japan."

"But...what does that have to do with my birthday party?" I ask. I am so confused.

"He thinks that all this bad stuff that's happened to us is your fault," he says quietly, almost whispering.

"What?" Something at his dad's company is my fault? "I didn't do anything! I don't even know what your dad does!"

"I know! I'm sorry, this isn't coming out right." He takes another deep breath. "He thinks that everyone got sick because of Asians and now he may be out of work because of them. He didn't know I was listening and he didn't tell me not to go to your party, but I don't want to upset him when he's already feeling so low."

All of the joy over my birthday drains out of me. All thoughts of parties and spelling bees disappear from my head. "What about you?" I ask. "Do you feel the same way?

That Asians are the bad guys?" I feel like this is the most important question I have asked in my life.

"No! I...I dunno."

"Oh." My insides feel weird, like there's a pit in my stomach. My eyes start to water. "That's disappointing." I start to turn away, then I think better of it. "You know what, it's more than disappointing. It's stupid." I'm so mad that I want to grab Josh's balled up lunch and stomp on it. I want to shake him and make him look at me. If he wants to stop being friends, the least he could do is look me in the eye and tell it to my face. "What about Mr. Chu? He's the best teacher we've ever had. Are you gonna switch out of his class?" I ask, my voice rising with anger.

"I don't know, Olive," Josh says quietly.

Somehow that makes me even more mad. "You know what? Don't even worry about not coming to my party—you are officially uninvited!"

I wish there were a door I could slam, but I have to settle for stomping my way to the lunchroom. I angrily swipe at the tears that finally escape, and for the first time that I can remember, I don't really care what my mom has packed me for lunch.

Chapter 8

I can't seem to concentrate on anything, and the rest of the afternoon passes in a blur. First Mrs. Ly gets knocked into the street for no reason, then I learn that some of Ben's friends had nasty things and words thrown at them. His *Asian* friends. Do lots of people feel the same way that Josh's dad does?

I gather my things and walk the four blocks home in a daze. I'm lucky I didn't get run over by a car or something. I take off my shoes, head straight to my room, and flop face down on my bed. I blindly feel around until my fingers brush my stuffed pony and pull it tightly to myself. Wishful Thinking Pony is a character from my favorite show, whose magic power is to be able to grant one wish each day. I wish that this day never happened.

"Olive, is that you?" my mom calls from the kitchen. Her footsteps come up the stairs and a second later, she pops her head into my room. "No after-school snack today? Are you already full up from Kandy Korner?" she teases.

"Mrmph," I say.

"Olive, are you okay?" Mom sits down on my bed.

I turn over onto my back. "I didn't go. I forgot."

"But you were so looking forward to it!" she exclaims. "You've been talking about it for weeks."

"I know," I say. "I just didn't feel like it anymore." I turn on my side and curl up like a shrimp. My voice starts to tremble. "I didn't have the best day."

Mom brushes the hair from my eyes. "Tell me."

So I do. "Why do people hate us?" I whisper when I finish.

"Oh, Olive," she says. "I'm sorry this has happened to you. I'd so hoped it wouldn't."

"What do you mean?" I ask.

She takes a hold of my hand. "These kinds of problems aren't new. Sometimes, people get scared or suspicious of other people. People who look or act or sound different from them. And when bad things happen, sometimes it feels easier to blame this other group, or..." Mom looks thoughtful, "to have someone to blame that isn't yourself, anyway. Not necessarily Asians. Just any other group of people who have a different skin color or don't speak the same language."

She rubs my back in soothing circles. "When I was a girl, there weren't many Asians in our neighborhood or at school. There was just me and another boy in another grade. We stuck out, and every now and then I would hear a comment. People speaking gibberish words at me to mimic how they thought I spoke."

I sit up at this. I can't stand the thought of anyone being mean to my mom.

"I never said anything back, never stood up for myself. I just ignored it and moved on as if their laughter didn't hurt. But it must have, because even after all these years, I still remember." Mom shudders a little, as if shaking off the memories. "Things are so different now, and just in your class, there are kids from so many different backgrounds and religions. You even have an Asian cowboy teacher!"

I give a small chuckle, even though I'm still thinking about what Mom said. It makes me sad to think that these things have been happening for so long, and I wonder if they've been happening around me too, and I just haven't noticed.

"I guess some things haven't changed enough," Mom continues. "But we can change how we respond. I don't think we can or should be quiet anymore. We shouldn't just accept being treated unfairly. Most importantly, you need to remember that none of this is your fault. You can't control how other people feel or act, but *you* are in charge of you. It's not your job to change anyone's mind or convince them of anything. Anyone worth knowing will see how amazing you are. So, continue being you. Continue being kind. To everyone."

She gives me a big squeeze and I feel some of the heaviness I've been carrying all afternoon leave my arms and legs. "Do you wanna walk me to school on Monday?" I peek at her from the cocoon of her arms. "I know you miss it, and I don't want you to have to quit cold turkey."

"Sure," she replies. "And after school, I'll even spring for a trip to Kandy Korner."

"Thanks, Mom. You're the best."

"I know." She grins. "But enough lazing about! I think your grandma could use a little help making the 100,000 spring rolls we need for your party."

Chapter 9

Normally, I would use my birthday as an excuse to get out of doing any chores, but I actually like helping Bà Nội in the kitchen.

I usually get stuck with the more boring tasks, like peeling carrots or chopping onions (the worst), but luckily, I see that my grandma has already done all the prep work and is on to the best part—the rolling!

Bà Nội already has a small mountain of rolls in front of her and nods toward a bowl full of what looks like chopped carrots, tofu, mushrooms, and noodles. "What's this?" I ask.

"For your vegetable friends," Bà Nội replies. She means vegetarian.

"Oh, cool." I love eating the meat-filled rolls, but touching raw meat is kinda gross. I peel a square wrapper from the stack on the counter and place it in front of me so that the square is now a diamond. I place a heaping spoonful of the filling near the bottom corner of the wrapper.

Bà Nội eyes my work. "Too much." I scoop some of the filling back into the bowl. "Good."

The bottom corner goes over the filling, then the sides, then I roll it up until it almost reaches the top corner. I dip my finger into the little bowl of mixed-up egg and water and use the goopy mixture like glue to seal my roll up tight. There are some bits poking out, but not a bad first effort, if I do say so myself.

"Bà Nội," I say as I unstick another wrapper from the pile, "can I ask you something?"

"Um hmm."

"Are you scared?"

"Why I scare?"

"You know, to go to the market. Since Mrs. Ly got hurt."

"Pfft. No, I not scare." Bà Nội keeps assembling her spring rolls like a machine, each roll picture perfect.

I set another wrapper in front of me and sneak a peek at Grandma. "But Mom always takes you to the market now. I thought you were too scared to go by yourself."

"Bah. Your mom worry too much." She waves her hand dismissively, and I duck out of the way of her filling-covered fingers. "I not scare of one bad man.

"Before we come here, there was fighting in my country. Any day, soldiers with big guns could come to our house, take all of the things we work for, eat all of our food. That scary. So, we leave. We leave everything...our house, our store, our animals. We only take what we can carry. That scary."

"Whoa...and that's when you came here?" I ask.

"No, first we go to Indonesia. Everyone go on a small boat. Lot and lot of people.

No room to lie down. Sit or stand only. And then another boat come and they rob us."

"Another boat…you mean pirates?!" I gasp. "You were attacked by real, live pirates?!"

Bà Nội nods but keeps working. I get the feeling that it might be easier for her to relive the memories if she doesn't have to look at me. "Yes, pirates. First time, not so bad. They take everything, but Bà Nội hide some gold jewelry. I sew into clothes. But the pirates, they could see we hungry. We already run out of food and water. So they feed us before they go. The second time, they not as nice."

My jaw drops. Bà Nội was attacked by pirates *twice*? "How have I never heard about this?" I wonder what else my family has been keeping from me.

"You never ask Bà Nội." She places another completed spring roll on her pile. In the time that I've been helping, Bà Nội has made eighteen rolls to my one. "The second time, they see that we have nothing left, so they angry. They try to hit our boat. Try to sink it. But we too close to land. A helicopter fly over us and scare pirates away."

I'm sure this is not right, but I can't help but picture Grandma on a little rowboat with a giant pirate ship, black flag flying, bearing down upon her. "Wow, Bà Nội. How long did it take you to get to Indonesia?"

"Nine days," she says. "Then we stay on island for nine months. In refugee camp."

"Nine months!" I blurt. "That's almost a whole year of school! You really went through a lot to get here, Bà Nội."

"Yes, we have to," she replies. "No choice. No future if we stay." Grandma pauses and actually looks at me. "That why I no scare. Bà Nội no scare of one bad man. Pfft, man who push old lady, not even a man."

"So, you only go shopping with Mom because she's worried about you?" Grandma surprises me by shaking her head.

"When I go with your mom, you can go too. You like buy bun and candy, yes?"

I give Bà Nội a tight squeeze around her middle. "Thanks, Bà Nội." Her hands are still covered in goo, so she pats my head with her forearm.

Chapter 10

I can't stop thinking about everything that my grandma went through to start a new life for her family. She's basically a hero. My birthday doesn't really seem like that big a deal anymore. But since Mom and Bà Nội have put in so much work, I'm determined that my party will go down as the best party ever thrown. Everyone will be talking about it for the rest of the year! Well, everyone but Josh. He's been at every birthday party that I can remember, and it makes me sad to think that he'll miss this one.

My family and I arrive at Sky's the Limit! a little early so we can set up. We'd spent ages last night blowing up balloons that are now scattered all around the party room. I'd wanted kazoos for everyone, but Mom nixed that idea. She thinks that the party will be loud enough without them. I'm also not allowed to sprinkle glitter around the room like I'd planned. Apparently, after hosting hundreds of parties, Sky's the Limit! has decided they're strictly a no-glitter zone. No exceptions.

The food has been arranged on giant platters and looks so yummy. No surprise there, since I did choose the entire menu. I also got to select the cake, which is not actually a cake at all. This year I've got a tower of donuts! Mochi donuts, to stay on theme, of course.

I spot an empty table at the end of the room and set out a bunch of markers and stickers and glitter glue (don't tell Sky's the Limit!).

"What's that for?" Mom asks.

"You'll see," I reply as I make my way to the front door to wait for my friends. They should be here any minute. No surprise, Ella and her mom are the first.

"Happy birthday, Olive!" she calls out and runs to give me a hug. She holds up a shiny gift bag, tissue paper spilling out the top. "Where should I put your present?"

"Ahhh! Thank you! There's a table in the party room. You can hang out in there while I wait for the rest of the guests," I tell her.

After Ella, it seems that all my classmates arrive in one big group and I'm soon busy greeting everyone and directing them to the party room. That should be it, I think. As I'm about to head in myself, one more familiar car pulls into the parking lot. My stomach drops. It's Josh and his parents. Oh no. What did Mom do?

"Hi, Josh. Hi, Mr. and Mrs. Simpson."

"Hi, Olive. Happy birthday," says Mr. Simpson. "Josh, why don't you and your mom join the others. I'd like to have a word with Olive."

I gulp and look at Josh with wide eyes. His shrug is not as reassuring as he intends it to be. Mr. Simpson waits until we're alone, while I shift awkwardly from foot to foot. Adult talks are the worst, and I'm crossing my fingers that someone will come save me. Mom must have heard about our meeting 'cause she pokes her head into the room and gives me a thumbs-up. No help there.

"Olive, I understand that Josh told you that he couldn't come to your party because of me," Mr. Simpson begins slowly. Whatever he wants to tell me, it doesn't seem like it's easy for him to say. "While that's not entirely true—you two have been friends for a long time, and I don't want that to stop—I'm ashamed to say that the other things he told you are."

"Oh," I say, looking outside at the parking lot, as if I were waiting on more guests to arrive. Anything to avoid meeting Mr. Simpson's eyes. "So, you think Asians are bad people?"

"No. You may not believe me right now, but I don't think that at all," he replies. "When your mom called to ask why Josh wasn't coming to the party and explained what he had told you, my heart broke. I did say those things, and for that I am deeply sorry. I was upset and lashed out at an easy target. Frankly, I was being pretty stupid. I didn't know that Josh had heard me, but I'm almost glad that he did."

At this, my eyes whip back to face him. How could this possibly be a good thing?

"I'm not at all happy that I almost ruined your friendship, but this incident has taught me that words matter. More than I ever thought. I don't expect you to forgive me right away, and I certainly don't want you to forget, but I do hope that you'll give me a chance to make things right."

I look at Mr. Simpson, at his eyes that have only ever before shown me kindness and laughter. I don't see anything that would make me doubt him, and I realize that I don't want to be angry. If Mr. Simpson is going to try to be better, I'm not going to stand in his way.

"Okay," I finally say, "but it did make me really sad. And you really don't get any more passes."

"That sounds fair," says Mr. Simpson. "Now, I hear there's a lot of fantastic food in the other room. What do you say, should we make sure the others haven't eaten everything without us?"

"Impossible. You know my mom always makes sure there's enough to feed an army!"

Chapter 11

We're all assembled in the party room, the kids waiting for the official go-ahead to run into the main room where all the trampolines and pits and nets are set up, and the adults trying to keep the kids from filling their bellies before they start jumping. But before we all get set loose, I get up onto a chair and take a deep breath.

"Thank you everyone for coming to my party," I announce. "I just want to take a minute to tell you about something that's been on my mind." I can see that everyone is itching to get bouncing, but they quiet down. I *am* the birthday girl, after all.

"It's about my grandma's friend, Mrs. Ly. Mrs. Ly went to Chinatown last week to get some groceries, just like she does all the time. Just like my grandma does all the time, too. But on this day, a stranger knocked into her and pushed her into the road. He didn't stop, he didn't even look back. Luckily, there were other people around who were able to help her. But she's very shaken and upset and is afraid to go back to Chinatown by herself again. She doesn't have any family here, so I thought we might cheer Mrs. Ly up by showing her that we care."

I point to the table I'd set my art supplies on earlier. "I've started a big card for Mrs. Ly that anyone can sign if they'd like to. It'll be there the whole time we're here, so if you're taking a break, maybe you can write her a note or draw her a picture. But for now, let's jump!"

After two circuits around the trampoline park—free jump, pit jump, basketball jump, and jump dodgeball—I'm ready for a breather. "I'm gonna get some water!" I yell to Penny, and she waves me off. I aim for the party room to get a drink and maybe a snack. Just a little one—I don't want too much in my stomach when I still have so much jumping to do. I ignore the veggie tray that I did not ask for and pick up a piece of California roll. Now seems like a good time to peek at Mrs. Ly's card.

I'm so happy to see that it's almost completely full! Andy, the best artist in our class, has drawn a border of flowers around the inside. There are too many hearts and well wishes to count. Someone has even left their phone number and offered to pick up groceries for her or to take her shopping! And in the corner, I see Mr. Simpson's "So sorry this happened to you, hope you have a speedy recovery."

Ben comes to stand beside me and gives me a little bump with his shoulder. "You did good, Olive. Mrs. Ly's going to really love this card."

"You think so? I know it's not much," I say, doubtfully.

"Sure it is," he replies. "Like you said earlier, Mrs. Ly needs to know that there are people out there who care. We can't solve all the world's problems in a single day, but I think every little bit we do helps."

Ben starts refilling snack bowls. "Oh, and guess what? Your friend Josh's dad saw some of the posters I put up around the neighborhood. He said he didn't know that kids were getting hassled and has offered to donate a hundred whistles to the Association. We can hand them out to anyone who's feeling a bit nervous about walking around alone."

"That's so great!"

I'm glad that Mr. Simpson is keeping his word and showing that he's a friend. Maybe he wouldn't have even noticed the posters if everything with Josh hadn't happened. All of the work that the Asian Students Association is doing, the donated whistles, and even Mrs. Ly's card—I have to believe that they're going to help make our community feel safer. And as much as it pains me to admit, I think Ben is right. Even if we think what we each do might not matter, it really does. Everything adds up. Everything counts.

Chapter 12

Our time at Sky's the Limit! is almost up, and I look around with satisfaction. Almost everyone is sweaty and flushed after jumping and running around for hours. And after stuffing their faces, they all look like they're ready for a nap. This party is going to be pretty hard to beat.

"Olive," my mom taps me on the shoulder, "your friends are starting to leave. Don't forget to hand out the goody bags."

I station myself by the table by the door

where we've laid out all the red gift bags. I got to pick out all the goodies myself, so I'm pretty confident they're going to be a hit. White Rabbit candies and Pocky; little baggies of shrimp crackers; and a pair of chopsticks to practice picking up the jelly beans I've also included. And since I was born on the year of the dragon, a sheet of shiny dragon stickers.

Penny, Ella, and Mia gather around me for a group hug. "Happy birthday, Olive!" they all chime.

"Your party was amazing!" says Ella. "So much fun!"

Mia clutches her stomach. "I'm so full."

"Mission accomplished." I grin. Bà Nội chooses that moment to glide past us, handing each of my friends a plate of rolls that she has already packed up to go.

"Yessss! Thank you!"

We all wave goodbye and promise to check into our online chat group later tonight. There's only one guest left. Josh.

"Hey," I say.

"Hey. I'm really sorry about what happened yesterday." He must be nervous because he's twisting the bottom of his T-shirt into knots.

"Yeah, me too," I reply. "I'm sorry I uninvited you."

"That's okay. I deserved it. I'm glad your mom called my mom."

"I figured she must have. Moms, right?" I shrug.

"Yep." He grimaces. "My mom was not happy when she got off that call. And she let my dad know it."

"Oof, sorry," I say.

"No, everything's fine now. We got to talk it all out."

"Double oof. You had to sit through a parent talk." I punch him softly on the arm.

"It wasn't so bad," he says, and I scoff. "Really," he adds. "But I did catch a bit of flack for eavesdropping. Anyway, I promise to do better."

"At not eavesdropping?" I ask.

"C'mon, let's be real, adults talk so loudly!" I nod in agreement, and he grins. Then he sighs. "I'm gonna try not to jump to conclusions. And to trust my gut. If it doesn't feel right, it probably isn't."

"And to always be nice to your best girl friend?" I say. Josh looks startled. "Friend that's a girl, I mean," I add quickly.

"I'll try...but you have to make the same promise, then," he says.

"Pfft. I'm already an awesome friend. Easy peasy," I reply.

"And we'll both call each other out when the other is being dumb."

"Deal," I say, and we shake hands.

"Oh, I have something for you." He digs in his front pocket.

"You do? You already got me a copy of *The Case of Windy Lake*. I've been wanting to read that forever!"

"It's just something small. Sammy helped me make it."

Josh holds out his closed fist. There's a small tinkle as he drops his gift in my extended hand.

"A friendship bracelet?" I ask. I turn it around to read the word spelled out in letter beads. "Physical?"

He grins. "So you won't forget how to spell it next time."

"Ugh, you're supposed to be nice to me!" I shove a goody bag at him.

"Happy birthday, Olive."

"Thanks, Josh." I slip the bracelet onto my wrist.

Chapter 13

Later that night, I arrange my pillows just as I want them and snuggle under my Magic Sparkle Fairy Ponies comforter. Wishful Thinking Pony is in her usual spot tucked under my arm, and I'm about to crack open my new book when my mom pops into my room.

"Good day?" she asks.

"The best," I reply. "Thanks for the party, Mom."

"You're very welcome, sweetie." Mom sits on my bed and tucks me and Pony in tight. "That was a very thoughtful thing you did for Mrs. Ly today. You can give it to her when we visit tomorrow morning."

"And maybe a goody bag?" I suggest. "I think Mrs. Ly likes sweets."

"Good idea," says Mom.

She gets up and is almost out of my room when I ask, "Why didn't you tell me that you'd called the Simpsons?"

Mom stops and turns back to face me. "I didn't tell you because I didn't know how things were going to pan out." She leans against my doorframe. "We've known the Simpsons for a long time, so I hoped that it was all a misunderstanding, but I wasn't sure. I know you're ten now, but you'll always be my baby, and I will spare you any hurt whenever I can, for as long as I can. Things may not always work out the way we want them to, but I'm glad they did this time."

Until the last few days, I've never really noticed that things were being kept from me. Things that my family thought were too scary or sad for me to know. But maybe turning ten is not just about unsupervised trips to the corner store. Maybe getting older also means being trusted to understand some of the difficult things that may be happening around me—and even to help! As one of my favorite superheroes once said, "With great power comes great responsibility."

"I'm glad that things worked out, too." I scootch back under the covers. "G'night, Mom."

"Goodnight, Olive." She turns away again and stops. "Did you remember to brush your teeth?"

"Yes, Mom."

Mom looks at me and doesn't say a word. One second. Two seconds. Three seconds. I get out of bed. "I'll brush them now."

"Good girl," she says. "Love you."

"G'night, Mom. Love you."

About the Author

Phuong Truong grew up in Ottawa and dreamed of being a rock star, a lawyer, or an author. She is pleasantly surprised to have achieved one of these goals. Her first book, *Everyone is Welcome*, was published in 2023. She works in book publishing and lives with her family in Toronto, Ontario.

Get in touch with Phuong on Instagram!
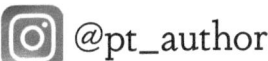 @pt_author